A Knight's Protection

Laurel O'Donnell

My Dear Reader –

I hope you enjoy Lia and Kade's story. They got swept up in the Templar knight treasure. No one knows for certain what happened to the fabled treasure, but I thought it would be fun if each knight was given part of the treasure to protect. This is the story of a Templar knight who died trying to protect the treasure, as I'm sure many of them did.

After you read A Knight's Protection, and if you feel so inclined, I would appreciate if you left a review to help other readers decide if they should read Lia and Kade's tale.

Don't forget to subscribe to my newsletter for updates on my newest novels, fun contests and so much more! https://www.laurel-odonnell.com

Without further ado, I bring you A Knight's Protection!

Welcome to my world!

CHAPTER ONE

England
October 18, 1307

The wind tumbled in with the storm and the small cruck creaked and groaned. For a moment, Lia thought the wattle and daub on the walls of the small house would blow in around them.

"The hens, child. The hens," Maeve called from her spot near the hearth.

Lia glanced at her as she hurried toward the door of the cruck. Maeve's old body hunched over the pot she stirred, her wrinkled hand slowly dragging the large wooden spoon round and round in the black kettle. The hearth fire snapped around the pot. Maeve swiped a strand of her gray hair from her forehead as she stepped back, lifting the ladle to her lips.

Lia paused before the door. "Will you be all right?"

Maeve huffed. "Better than those hens, if you don't hurry."

Lia grinned and opened the door. A rush of wind jerked the door hard, blowing in fiercely and scattering Maeve's herbs across the wooden table in the center of the room. Lia hunched her shoulders and ducked her head against the strong wind.

"Don't forget Firefoot!" Maeve called, hurrying to the table to hold down what remained of the herbs.

Lia nodded and pulled the door closed behind her. She looked out over the yard. The familiar landscape was a strange shade of gray. Dark clouds churned in the sky, moving toward the cruck. She raced around to the side of the house where the hen house she had built years ago was situated. Her theory had been that the cruck would offer the hen house protection from the elements and so far that theory had proven correct. Lia hoped it would continue to do so.

A KNIGHT'S PROTECTION

A gust of wind pushed her toward the fence around the hen house. She opened the gate and it blew out of her hand, slamming against the fence.

Lia rushed to the hen house, bending, and peering in through the small opening. She held her hair out of her eyes as she glanced about the small house. Most of the hens were huddled on their nests. She counted them as her hair blew wildly around her shoulders. "One, two, three…" One was missing. Mrs. Duckworth. She cursed silently to herself, knowing Maeve would not be pleased if she said the curse aloud. She withdrew from the small window, scanning the small enclosure outside the hen house for Mrs. Duckworth. Lia saw the small, crazy white bird huddled and squawking distraughtly in a corner. She ran to the hen and picked it up, huddling it against her, whispering softly to it.

A rumble of thunder rolled across the darkening sky and Mrs. Duckworth flapped her white wings in fear. Lia held the hen tightly to her chest, so it wouldn't fly off, and hurried to the hen house. The wind suddenly strengthened. It pushed her hard and she almost slammed into the hen house. She managed to bend down, shielding Mrs. Duckworth, and shoved the hen inside the house.

Mrs. Duckworth squawked and hopped into the protection of the house. Lia closed the small wooden door on the hen house and stood quickly. Her hair whipped madly in the wind and she pushed it aside to look for Firefoot. A large bolt of lightning speared the sky and Lia cringed as the white hot jagged strip of light slashed the sky. She hurried from the hen enclosure, closing the gate, and latching it behind her.

A huge crack of thunder made her jump. It was dangerous to be out in this weather. She had to find Firefoot. She clicked her tongue and yelled his name. But the black mare did not appear.

Lia held her hair back from her forehead as she looked west to the copse of trees there, then to the east and the clearing. There was no sign of Firefoot. She called the horse again, knowing she couldn't be far. Not in weather like this. She followed the dirt road, calling her name, clucking her tongue. The rumble of the thunder and the roar of the wind made it hard to hear her own voice and she was afraid the horse wouldn't hear her calls.

With no sign of Firefoot, concern gnawed at Lia's mind. The mare never wandered this far away. A large round drop of rain hit the earth beside her.

Suddenly, she spotted a shadow in a group of trees near the side of the road. It wasn't far from the main road, farther than Firefoot had ever wandered, but at least she had found her. With relief, Lia raced over to the horse, crashing through the bushes that hid her. With a gust of wind and rumble of thunder, the sky opened, and rain fell in large drops, but the thick branches overhead protected her from the full brunt of the rain.

Lia reached for the shadow. "Firefoot, I thought…" Her words faded as she realized this horse was not her mare. The horse before her was large and looked at her with disdain. She stepped back, and her heel hit something. She almost fell, but caught herself and turned.

The sky lit with lightning, and in the dappled light it cast she got a quick view of a man in a white tunic laying on the ground. She gasped and stepped away from him. She bumped into the horse and the animal neighed in an annoyed burst of sound, but it remained where it was. For a moment, she felt trapped between the man and the horse. Rain continued to fall all around them outside the protection of the trees. The wind pushed a fine mist towards them, coating her, the horse, and the prone man. As she waited, the man remained still. Suspiciously still. Was he sleeping? "I'm sorry to disturb you."

Still, no response. She scowled. Maybe he was sleeping and had not heard her. Prickles ran across the nape of her neck. Thunder rumbled in the sky as the rain pelted the leaves of the trees and the earth around them. A few tiny droplets of rain managed to get through the overhead leaves to drip onto his face, yet he did not move.

Lia glanced toward the road. Was he alone?

He moaned, and she glanced back at him.

When a spear of lightning tore through the sky, Lia saw the man's arm wrapped tightly around his torso, his hand holding his side, clutching it. She dropped to her knees at his side. "Are you hurt?"

The man peeled away his arm.

Two things struck Lia. His palm was covered in red liquid she knew was blood and his white tunic had a red cross on it. It was a symbol she had seen before. The man was a Templar knight. She looked up towards his face.

His features were hidden in the darkness of the canopy of trees. "What happened?" She moved his arm aside and saw his side was stained with red. She moved closer to inspect his wound and her knee settled into a thick moist spot of oddly warm earth beside him. She touched her knee and lifted her fingers. More blood. This was not good.

She couldn't treat him here in the dark. She had to get him back to Maeve. She attempted to get him to sit up by pulling his shoulder. "Come."

"No," he whispered in a choked, pained voice.

"I can help you."

"No one can help me now." He signaled his horse with a jerk of his head. "Ale."

Lia was shocked at his denial for aid; at his willingness to die. Was he mortally wounded with no intent of fighting for his life? She stood and moved to his horse where she found a flask tied to the horn of his saddle. She untied it and returned to his side. She helped him sit up, cushioning his head in her arm, and brought the flask to his lips.

He drank deeply and then pushed the flask from his mouth. "Who are you?"

Lia hesitated. She and Maeve lived on the outskirts of the village. The people of the village didn't trust them and didn't like them because of the potions Maeve created. Only when the peasants and commoners had trouble, and had no one else to turn to, did they seek them out for help. A tonic for pain relief. A concoction for a sick animal. A syrup for an incurable cough. Lia held no embarrassment for what Maeve did or what Maeve taught her, she simply had to be cautious. "I live up the road with Maeve."

"The alchemist?" he asked.

"Healer," Lia corrected with a small smile. Some people called them witches behind their backs and Lia was certain her red hair contributed to this label. "Maeve can help you, I'm certain."

He shook his head stubbornly. His body tensed whenever he breathed in. Not a good sign. Thunder rumbled around them.

"How did this happen?" Lia wondered. "Who did this to you?"

"There are many who want us dead," he whispered. He reached beneath his tunic and pulled out a piece of parchment. He stared at it for a long moment, his jaw clenched. Then, he shoved it toward her.

Lia hesitantly took the parchment. Confusion washed over her as she stared at the foreign letters. "I can't read."

The knight chuckled, and blood spluttered from his lips. He sighed back into her arms. "Hide it. Protect it." He grabbed her arm, squeezing it. "The Lord has brought you to me. You must take care of this."

Lia looked down at the parchment. Maeve could read it.

"Don't let anyone find it. Don't show it to anyone."

Lia frowned. "Why? What does it say?"

He released her arm and settled back. "Resist its temptation." He sighed. "What is your name?"

"Lia."

"I'm sorry to have to leave this burden with you, Lia. I would give anything not to. But I'm afraid my time on this earth is over. And this is important. Very important."

Burden? Lia glanced at his wound. "Let me treat your wound. I can help with the pain."

"The pain is a punishment that I willingly endure."

Lia ignored his words. She placed the parchment on his chest and eased his white tunic up to see the slash in his side. "It's a sword wound." Her mind was already working on what she needed to treat it.

"They will come for you if they know you have it. Don't tell anyone about it."

Lia scowled and looked into his face. Lines of concern etched his brow. Wrinkles creased the corners of his eyes and mouth. "Who will come? Why do they want it? What is it?"

"It is your responsibility now. Hide it. Tell no one of it and you will be safe." He winced and then closed his eyes. "God be with you, child."

"Wait, wait!" Lia cried. "I can help you!"

His hand tightened around hers. "You already have."

Thunder cracked overhead, and the knight breathed his last.

Lia stared at him. He was gone. She released him, easing his head to the ground and sat back. The horse neighed behind her. She picked up the parchment to look at it again. What was written on it? It must be very important. She tucked it into her chemise to keep it dry and stood. She looked at the horse. He stared at her as if judging.

Maeve always said animals housed part of their owners in their hearts. The horse watched her, silently. She wasn't sure whether she believed that or not. Either way, she couldn't very well leave it alone out here in the dark forest. She took its reins. "Easy," she whispered.

The rain seemed to have let up a little. It wasn't the downpour of a few moments ago. She stepped forward, out from the protective overhang of the branches of the trees. No, it wasn't raining as hard and the dark sky was giving way to muted light. She glanced back at the knight. She would tell Maeve about him and then ride into town to find the bailiff after she found Firefoot.

She pushed her wet hair from her forehead. After everyone was taken care of, she would decide what to do with the parchment.

CHAPTER TWO

Lightning flashed in the windows of the Great Hall, illuminating the dark room in bursts of light. Kade de Claremont sat in a chair on the far side of the hall, watching his father pace back and forth, watching the man who haunted his nightmares for the past five years. His father was tall and brash, his fists always clenched. The hearth smoldered behind the old man, casting a dim red glow around him. Kade grimaced in hatred and stretched his feet out before him, his hand wrapped around a mug of ale.

When his older brother Ralf, heir to de Claremont as Kade had constantly been reminded growing up, came in soaking wet from the storm, Kade couldn't help smiling. Better Ralf in the rain following Father's orders than him. Ralf had always been the good son, following his father's orders. Kade lifted his mug to his lips and drank deeply.

Ralf crossed the room, his booted feet crunching on the rushes on the floor. He stopped before his father. He had grown taller in the five years Kade was gone. His brother stood almost equal to his father's height. Kade liked that his brother's stature had grown; perhaps that would give him more courage to fight back against their father's cruel treatment.

"You found him?" his father demanded.

Kade waited to hear the words that would either condemn or exonerate his brother.

Ralf shook his head. "There was a fight. He killed Sir Roland."

A fight! Now that was something that interested Kade. He looked down into his mug of ale, feigning disinterest, but keeping his ears tuned to the conversation.

"I don't care who he kills. I want him, alive," his father growled.

"He was wounded, father," Ralf explained. "He couldn't have gotten far."

"Then what are you doing here? Find him. Bring him to me."

Lightning lit the night sky as Ralf hesitated. "The men were weary. They needed rest."

Kade cringed. Ralf was always worried about the men's well-being. One day, he would make a good lord, but not today.

Ralf's answer was not at all what his father wanted to hear. Kade lifted his gaze to the two men. His father stood like stone facing Ralf, his fists clenched, glaring at his son. Ralf's brown-haired head was bent. Ralf knew what was coming. He knew his father was displeased. His father's rage was coming and still, he stood there, willing to take it.

Every nerve, every fiber, tightened in Kade's body in preparation. Get out of there, Ralf, Kade mentally commanded.

Ralf stood stoically. Perhaps out of fear, perhaps out of pride.

His father swung his fist, connecting with Ralf's cheek. Ralf stumbled back. The effect wasn't enough for his father; he landed another blow to Ralf's jaw. "You worthless, cowardly dog."

Kade rose to his feet, coming out of the darkness. "It won't help."

His father whirled, and Ralf looked at him.

"It's already done," Kade said. "Beating Ralf won't undo it."

His father's shock disappeared as Kade approached him like a storm cloud, crossing the expanse of the Great Hall. "The prodigal son slinks home," he mocked.

Kade grinned. "I came when news of mother reached me. At least she is at peace now, away from you."

"She was weak."

"She was a woman. She shouldn't have had to stand against your fists."

"It took you an entire week to face me, to tell me that? Too afraid?" His father's face filled with scorn.

Kade met Ralf's gaze over his father's shoulder. This was a scene that had played out between them many times before. Too many times. It was why Kade had left in the first place. "Too contemptuous."

"You impudent –" His father lifted his fist.

Kade tensed his body, but he wasn't surprised by his father's reaction. This was the exact welcome he had expected.

"Father," Ralf called, stilling the blow. "I will take a new squad of guards to look for de Rolleston."

His father glared at Kade for a long moment, his upper lip twitching, his fist lowering. "You do that."

Behind his father, Kade saw Ralf move toward the entrance, leaving him alone with his father. Some things didn't change.

His father glowered at Kade for a moment longer.

Kade had expected the hatred burning in his eyes. He expected a beating, or at the very least an attempted beating. His father turned away from him, and approached the hearth. His back was arched, his steps were slow. Kade scowled. What he didn't expect was to suddenly see his father as tired and old. It pleased him. But not enough. "Can't even catch one knight? You must be losing your touch."

His father fell into a chair, his hands closing over the arms. "You think you can do better? You? A sniveling, milk-witted scut. Ha!"

"I could find him." Kade felt obliged to announce. He knew he could find the man if he put his mind to it. But he had no desire to help his father. His father ruled by fear and rage. Men didn't want to please him, not even his sons.

His father laughed, the shrill sound echoing through the Great Hall.

It grated Kade's nerves. He remembered how his father laughed at him when he fell from a horse when he was five, remembered how he laughed when the first arrow he shot flew over the target, remembered how he laughed when he cut himself sparring with another boy. The horrid sound of his father's vile laugh rang in his ears, echoing through his memories.

Suddenly, his father's laughter stopped. "You think you can find him? Then do it. Stop wasting my time."

Kade's lip curled. He had no intention of doing his father's bidding. Ever again. Kade walked up to his father and stood beside him for a moment, staring into the embers of the hearth. "Did you kill Mother?"

Silence stretched. Kade knew his father was withholding the information on purpose. Kade wanted to know and his father wouldn't tell him. It gave his father power. Kade regretted asking him. He turned away.

"She fell," his father said coldly.

Kade paused for a moment, as if waiting for his father to add more to his statement.

"Clumsy girl," his father finally snarled with a chuckle.

Prickles danced across the nape of Kade's neck. Clumsy girl. His mother had "fallen" many times as he grew up. Every bruise, every cut, every broken bone was attributed to a fall or an accident. He felt a terrible guilt well up inside him. He was wise enough now to know that none of his mother's wounds had come from any accident. He should have stayed. He should have protected her. "What did you do to her?"

"Me?" his father cackled with joy. "She fell."

Sickened, it was all Kade could do not to run from his father. He whirled away from the old man and strolled out into the corridor, then turned the corner to head for the doors. All he wanted to do was be away from this place, from his father. He was surprised to find Ralf leaning against the wall, with his head down as if inspecting his boots.

"I didn't know you were here," Ralf said quietly.

"No," Kade agreed. No one had known except a few servants. He did not sleep in the castle, nor did he make himself known to anyone else. He wanted nothing to do with his old home. He had only returned to pay respects to his mother.

Ralf lifted his gaze and there was pain and apology in his brown eyes. "I'm sorry, Kade. Truly. I didn't know where you were to send word about mother."

Kade shrugged, but his lips thinned. "Word reached me. What happened to her?"

Ralf looked away again. "They had a terrible argument. About this de Rolleston." He shook his head. "Mother lost."

Kade clenched his teeth. He should have been here to protect his mother. And his brother. "Things haven't changed."

"Father hasn't changed."

"Was her death quick?" Kade asked, imagining his sweet, loving mother's kind face twisted in pain.

Ralf hesitated. "No. It took a week for her to pass."

Kade closed his eyes to fight back the anguish and regret.

"I did everything I could for her, Kade. Everything. It was almost like every bone in her body was broken. She would cry out and there was nothing I could do to help her."

His brother's words mirrored Kade's sentiments exactly. There had been nothing he could have done differently to protect her. She would not listen to reason when he had told her to leave. She said she loved his father. She vowed she would never abandon no matter what. And Kade knew he couldn't stay. He looked up at Ralf. "And you? Is it better for you?"

Ralf shrugged slightly. "I try to stay away from him as much as I can. And he is getting older."

They stood in awkward silence for a long moment, each not knowing what to say to the other. Kade knew there were a thousand things he wanted to say to his older brother. He was sorry he didn't ask him to come away with him. But he hadn't been sure how he was going to survive by himself, let alone if he had Ralf to take care of. And somewhere inside of him, he had hoped that Ralf would be able to protect their mother.

He had been wrong. So very wrong.

CHAPTER THREE

Lia reached the village early the next morning. The sun was just rising over the horizon, bathing the lands in an early golden glow. The Templar knight's war horse she rode trudged through the muddy road, kicking up large clumps of slick earth from the recent rains. She had always been a good rider and had few problems controlling the war horse.

The village was slowly coming to life, peasants emerging from shops to open doors, tossing used water into the streets.

Lia dismounted before the only inn in the village. She entered the main room. It was dark. A dying fire in the hearth cast little illumination over the room. Two tables lined the wall near the hearth. She paused as she saw two young men,

Bors and Elias, arguing over something near one of the tables. Bors was large, a foot taller than Elias. His dark, greasy hair hung to his shoulders in an uneven line. Elias shoved Bors, but it didn't move him. Elias was the smaller of the two and the instigator, telling Bors what to do. His black hair was knotted and unkempt. They glanced up at Lia when she entered. A sly grin split Bors's lips, making the cut on his cheek ooze.

Lia could have helped him with a salve to place over the cut, but she didn't like the two men. Every time she came into town, they looked at her with lewd gazes that made her uncomfortable.

Her gaze quickly moved by them to see a shadowed man sitting in the corner, a customer, she surmised.

On an adjacent wall, the wall to her left, a man was bent stirring something in a pot over a second hearth. Joy bubbled inside of her. Ned was one of the few friends she had in the village. She and Maeve had once eased his daughter's stomach pain and for that he was grateful and treated them kindly. She quickly moved up to Ned. "Good day, Ned," she greeted.

Ned stood, wiping his hands on his apron. A genuine grin touched his lips as seeing her. "Good day, Lia!" He was as tall as she was with a round stomach.

"Have you seen Bailiff Samuelson?" she wondered.

"No, I'm sorry. I haven't seen him today. He hasn't come in yet." Ned cast a disapproving glare at the pair of men watching them before he leaned in close to whisper, "You'd best leave before there is trouble. They're both in rare moods today, but they just paid for their meals, so I can't make them leave."

Lia glanced at Bors and Elias and nodded. "Thank you, Ned." She headed for the door.

Elias raced around her, stepping before the door to block her path. "Come, now, Lia. That's rude. Ya didn't even say hello to us!" His breath stunk like rotted fish.

"We saw ya come into town with that war horse," Bors said from behind her. "Where'd ya get it?"

Lia lifted her chin, but before she could answer, Bors continued. "Do you like how it feels between yer legs?" Both men chuckled and Bors moved to Elias's side, nudging him with his elbow.

"That's no way to talk to a lady." The voice came from the darkness of the corner table.

Lia turned. She was surprised to see the customer slowly rising from a chair.

"When I see one, I'll speak better," Elias answered with a sideways grin.

"Then you are blind as well as daft," the man said. That erased Elias's humor.

As the man behind the voice came into the light of the hearth, Lia saw he wore a sword strapped to his waist. His brown jupon and leggings had no holes. He was a nobleman, she was certain.

Elias and Bors must have come to the same conclusion because their demeanor suddenly changed. Their heads bowed slightly, and they nodded, backing toward the door. "Apologies, m'lord," Elias mumbled.

"Not to me. To her."

Elias grimaced. "Apologies, Lia."

Lia nodded, knowing how much effort and embarrassment the apology caused Elias.

Bors quickly opened the door and the two almost tripped over each other as they ran from the inn.

Lia couldn't take her gaze from the lord. His dark, shoulder-length hair fell forward. His jaw was square and rugged, his face clean-shaven. His nose was straight and chiseled. His deep blue eyes bore into her. He looked familiar to her, but she couldn't place him.

"They shouldn't treat you like that."

"They always do," Ned exclaimed. "It's disgraceful!"

Lia shrugged. "It doesn't bother me."

The man pulled a chair out and indicated she sit in it. "Ale," he ordered Ned.

Lia had no coin to spend on ale. She took the offered seat, but shook her head. "No, Ned. I don't need ale."

The man laughed as he took a seat in the chair opposite her. "I do."

Ned nodded and hurried to the hearth.

"Is that your war horse those two were interested in?" the man wondered.

Lia shook her head. "No."

The man nodded. "You'd best be cautious someone doesn't steal him. Where did you find him?"

Lia scowled slightly. "I didn't say I found him."

He shrugged. "My apologies."

Lia squinted her eyes, trying to fathom why he looked so familiar. "Do I know you?"

"I am Kade de Claremont."

Her eyes widened slightly. Of course! His manner was commanding and confident, his back straight with pride. A flash of memory came to her about Kade de Claremont. It had been said that he had left the castle suddenly, under suspicious circumstances years ago. And then as she looked closer at him, she recognized his eyes. He had the same eyes as his mother, lady de Claremont. "I'm sorry about your mother."

Kade nodded, and looked away toward Ned.

"She loved you very much."

A scowl appeared on his brow and he turned those deep blue eyes back to her. "Why would you say such a thing?"

Startled by his confusion, Lia pulled back slightly. "It was apparent when she spoke of you."

"You knew her?"

Lia nodded. "Maeve and I ministered to her many times." Kade looked away, but not before Lia saw agony in his eyes. "I'm sorry if this causes you pain. I shouldn't speak of her."

"No," Kade insisted. "I'm sorry. At least you were there for her."

There was something in the way he said the words, something bitter. Lia thought it better she said nothing more, but there was one more thing she had to tell him. "I'm glad you are here. Your mother had a message for you. I was to give it to you if I ever saw you."

Kade's mouth dropped slightly open. "For me?"

Lia nodded. "I didn't think I would ever meet you or even see you. I'm glad I'm able to tell you. She said she loves you." His lips pursed, and Lia continued. "And forgives you."

Kade swallowed and lowered his head.

"She said…" Lia scowled, looking away from Kade, trying to remember. The last part of the message really made no sense to her, but lady de Claremont made her repeat the phrase three times. "Don't let them find him. They can't get it." Lia nodded. "Yes, that's what she said." She looked at Kade. "Don't let them find him. They can't get it."

Kade's head snapped up and locked gazes with Lia. "Find whom?"

"I'm sorry. I don't know. It took all her effort to tell me that."

Ned placed the ale on the table and Kade handed him coin. He appeared lost in thought and Lia stood to leave. "Thank you for your help with Bors and Elias. They mean no harm, but can be crude."

Kade stood immediately. "You are leaving?"

Sympathy washed over her. "I have to find the bailiff." She glanced outside, then backed to Kade.

Kade followed her gaze, then looked back to her. "Because of the war horse?"

Lia considered his question. This was lord de Claremont. The bailiff worked for him. Surely, she would be able to tell him. "The war horse belongs to a knight. He died sometime during the storm last night. I found him."

"Show me where."

Kade stared down at the dead knight. The red cross on his white tunic proclaimed him a Templar knight. This could be trouble. Kade knew King Philippe was pursuing and arresting all the Templar knights. He knew a dead Templar was nothing to the king. But what of his father? Was this the knight his father was searching for?

The knight's old, weathered face was peaceful, his eyes closed. He was just an old man. Kade's gaze scanned him. A slash mark and red liquid marred the white tunic near his abdomen. Kade was pretty certain this had been the fatal blow. The knight lay in a puddle of blood, the liquid having dripped down his side to pool on the ground. Kade remembered Ralf telling their father that there had been a fight. Could this really be the knight his father was searching for?

And then he remembered his mother's message from the girl, Lia. 'Don't let them find him. They can't get it.' He stared at the old man. Was this the man that had caused his mother's death? Was this the man Mother and Father had argued over? What had Ralf said his name was? De Rolleston. Kade's fists clenched as anger rolled through him. What was so important about this old knight to cause his mother to stand up to his father? "Did he say anything to you?" he growled.

After a moment of hesitation, Lia answered, "No. He was dead when I found him."

Frustrated, Kade bent and ran his hands over the knight's body, waving a few flies away that had started to congregate around the corpse. Perhaps the knight had something that was important, the 'it' of his mother's message. He searched again, slowly. He tucked his hands into the knight's belt, into his empty scabbard. He removed one of his boots and looked inside.

"What are you looking for?" Lia wondered.

Kade didn't answer. He had no idea what he was searching for. Maybe there was nothing here.

He removed the other boot and looked inside. Kade lifted the knight's tunic and then the knight's chainmail. Blood lined the old man's stomach. The gaping wound had stopped flowing. There was nothing hidden there. He sat back on his heels. "You found him like this?"

"Yes."

"Was anyone else around? Another knight?" He swiveled around to look at her. "Did you see anyone else?"

She shook her head, her red locks swaying over her shoulders in thick waves.

"Did you try to help him?"

"He was already dead when I found him."

Kade looked back at the knight and stood. There was nothing on him that might illicit the message from his mother. Whatever reason his father was searching for him so badly, died with the knight.

Kade turned to Lia. The sun shone down through the leaves of the tree, pooling her in a glorious glow of sunlight. His breath caught. Her red hair all but glowed like fire as the sun touched it. Her nose was pert, her lips slightly parted. His gaze was caught by her dress and the nicely rounded portion of her breasts. For a quick moment, his gaze swept her chest and the way the fabric pulled over it. The torso of her dark cotton dress was splattered with a small freckling of black dots. It took a moment for Kade to realize he had seen that type of spatter before, numerous times. From dying knights. Those small dots of blood came from a mouth expulsion, coughing or sneezing of a mortally wounded knight.

Could the spattering have come from Sir de Rolleston? Had he been alive when she found him? What could the old knight have told her to make her lie to him?

CHAPTER FOUR

Lia was grateful Father Stephen had given the knight a proper burial at the chapel. As a Templar knight, he deserved one.

She bent over the lavender growing in a field beside their cruck. She picked a few of the finest blooming stalks and paused to sniff one, loving the sweet scent. She still could not get her mind off Kade de Claremont. It was almost as though he had appeared out of nowhere. Tall and strong and so handsome. She remembered the way he looked at her with such intensity. Yes, he was stunning to behold, like a carved statue, but he was a noble man. He could marry anyone he wanted. He would never want her.

She shook herself from her musings. What was she thinking? Marriage? No one would marry her. Marriage was not in her future. She was resigned to a life alone, like Maeve. Still, she was grateful she had found Kade to give him lady de Claremont's message. He needed to hear it, she could tell. Hopefully, it had given him peace.

She lifted the lavender to her nose and inhaled deeply. Inside her dress, the edge of the parchment rubbed against the skin on her chest. The image of Kade searching the old Templar knight came to her mind. He had removed the dead man's shoes, searched his scabbard. He clearly had been looking for something.

Could it be the parchment the knight had given her? She had kept the parchment a secret, as the old knight had advised. She kept the parchment close to her, beneath her chemise so Maeve would not find it, even accidentally.

Last night, in the darkness, when she was laying on her cot waiting for sleep, she had taken it out and looked at it, angling it into a shaft of moonlight that shown in through one of the planks of wood on the roof. She could no more make out what was written on it then than she could the second time she looked at it this morning when Maeve was relieving herself. She didn't like to keep secrets from Maeve and the parchment was no exception. But she was not going to put Maeve in any danger.

She dropped to her bottom in the middle of the lavender, a poof of their scent engulfing her. She glanced around, making sure no one was watching. It seemed silly. She knew no one was watching, but the knight's warning was still fresh in her mind. She reached into her chemise and pulled the parchment out. It was all black squiggly lines to her; she couldn't read it. Maeve would be able to read it. Tempting as the thought was, she couldn't ask her. The knight had warned her not to show it to anyone.

The parchment seemed harmless enough. And she had this burning desire to know what was written on it.

She stared at the parchment. It was old, wrinkled by the passage of time. She ran a finger over the lines. What was written here that was worth dying over? There was one man in the village that Lia trusted enough to read it to her. Father Stephen. She just wanted to know what it said and then she would bury it so no one else would find it.

She forgave him. The words Lia had spoken to him played over and over in his thoughts. Kade didn't understand how his mother could forgive him when he would never forgive himself. Still, that wasn't what caused him the previous sleepless night. It was the other words she had spoken. 'Don't let them find him. They can't get it.' Find him? The dead knight? It had to be. That was what Ralf told him his mother and father were arguing about. His father hadn't found the knight, he did. But the second part of the message still confused him... 'They can't get it.' What did that mean? He had searched the fallen knight, but couldn't find anything worthy of protection.

He rubbed his eyes. There was one person at the center of all of it. Lia. She had found the dead knight. Had he given her something to protect? Even if he hadn't, Kade wanted to speak to her. He wanted to learn more about his mother, about what she said, every word. What kind of injuries she had. Why Lia couldn't save her. His heart twisted. He bowed his head over his morning meal of porridge.

The door opened and closed.

The brown-haired little girl who waited on him jumped up from the hearth in excitement. "Lia!" she greeted.

Kade looked up in time to see the child wrap her small arms around Lia's thin waist. Lia's red hair was wound tightly in a braid behind her back, but small stray locks had come free of the confinement, trailing down her slender neck. Kade's heart quickened at the sight of her small, but lithe form.

Lia embraced the girl tightly. "I brought you some lavender, Alice," she said.

"You did?" The child pulled back to look up at her.

Lia handed the girl a handful of purple stemmed flowers as Ned came in the front door carrying an arm full of fire wood. He smiled. "Good morn, Lia!"

"Good day to you, Ned."

Kade stood, drawing her attention. Surprise crossed her wide, large blue eyes before she approached him.

She put her hands behind her back. "I thought you would have returned to the castle."

He watched appreciatively the way her hips swayed before he acknowledged her words. "And miss Ned's ale? Never!"

Ned grinned.

In truth, Kade knew Ned was grateful for the patronage and the coin. And he had no desire to return to his father's castle. "What are you doing in the village?"

"I've brought flowers for the knight's grave."

"Do you mind if I accompany you?"

She shook her head. "Not at all." She waved to Alice who was inhaling the scent of the lavender, and Ned as he put the wood near the hearth, before heading for the door.

Kade held the door open for her.

He closed the door behind her and took up pace beside her. Her red hair shone in the bright sunlight. "I wanted to thank you for the message from my mother."

Lia nodded. "She was a kind woman."

Kade nodded, remembering the warmth in his mother's smile. "What kind of injuries did she have?"

Lia glanced at him, but remained silent.

"You said you ministered to her."

"M'lord –"

"Kade. Please."

Lia nodded. She looked away from him as if contemplating. "She was prone to…accidents."

Kade stiffened. His jaw clenched. "Is that what you ministered to her for?"

"There were many times I visited the castle over the last years. She fell. She hit her head. She even broke her arm once."

Kade clenched his fist. He hated his father, painfully aware that he was the primary cause of these so-named accidents. But he hated himself more. "I should have been there."

She gently touched his wrist. "Even if you were, there was nothing you could have done for her."

Even her gentle touch didn't soothe his guilty conscious. "I could have..." Kade stopped. "Protected her from... her falls."

"You couldn't have protected her all the time." Her gaze swept his face. "It would have been you instead of her and she would never have allowed that."

Kade reeled back, his mouth opened in surprise. Did she know the truth? Did she know it was his father's fists that had inflicted injury on his mother?

"I did my best to alleviate her pain," Lia said.

Guilt stabbed him in the chest. "Was she in a lot of pain?"

Sadness entered Lia's bright blue eyes. "Only this last time. I came every day for a week and it seemed she only got worse. No matter what I did."

Kade saw his agony mirrored in Lia's eyes. He wanted to embrace her for all she did for his mother. "I'm glad you were there for her."

She nodded. She touched the side of his face. "She loved you. She spoke of you often."

Her warmth seeped into skin. He let her comfort wash over him. "What did she say?"

"She told me stories of when you were young." She pulled her hand back from his face. "I'm sorry for being so familiar, but I feel like I know you."

Kade missed her touch the moment she withdrew it. He yearned for her to place her hand back on his face, to touch him again, to soothe him.

Lia stepped back, folding her hands before her. "Thank you for your help with the bailiff."

The moment was lost. She was apparently feeling quite awkward and Kade didn't know what to do to ease her.

"Why would someone want him dead? What could an old knight like him possibly have worth killing over?" Lia asked.

Kade shrugged. "King Philippe sent out an order to arrest all Templar knights. Perhaps he resisted."

Lia frowned. "Perchance. Or perchance he was carrying something." She looked up at him. "What were you looking for when you searched him?"

"Usually knights carry a coin purse. Since I couldn't find that, my guess is that he was robbed." Kade felt guilty for lying to her, but he wanted to protect her from whatever secret the knight hid. He didn't want her to get involved. His mother had died because of it.

She was silent, staring into his eyes with an intensity of disbelief that made him want to tell her the truth.

Suddenly, the thunder of horses pounding up the road caught their attention. Together, they stepped aside as a squadron of soldiers rode into the village. Kade saw his family's crest on the men's tunics and recognized Ralf leading the way.

When Ralf saw Kade, he reined in his horse to a stop before him. The other men rode on.

Ralf looked down at Kade, his stare stopping on Lia for a moment before continuing to his brother. "The bailiff said you found him."

Kade couldn't help noticing Ralf's eye was blackened and bruised. He nodded, and his teeth gritted, even as anger churned inside of him. His father had punished Ralf for not locating the knight first.

Ralf sighed and swung his leg over the side of his horse to dismount. "Father is furious."

Kade looked again at Ralf's blackened eye. "I could have guessed."

"Where is the knight?"

"We laid him to rest in the field near the church. It was too late, Ralf. He was already dead." Kade glanced at Lia. She looked down at the muddy road, allowing them to talk. He wondered if his brother knew she had found the body, and if he didn't when he would. The bailiff would not keep it a secret.

"Father wants his body."

Surprise rocked Kade. That seemed morbid, even for his father. Didn't Father believe he was the right knight? Or was there something more to this? "What is it, Ralf?" he demanded. "What's going on?"

Ralf stared at Kade for a moment as he chewed on his lower lip. Then, he shook his head and looked away. "I can't tell you."

He stepped closed to Ralf, hissing, "Mother died because of this. I'm going to find out."

Ralf sighed softly, relenting. He took a step away from Lia and Kade followed him. "It wasn't the knight Father was after," he said quietly so Lia wouldn't hear. "It was something he had on his person. A Templar treasure."

Templar treasure? There had never been any proof of Templar treasure, just rumors and whispered gossip. Had his father gone mad? Or had he discovered something? He felt a slight quickening in his heart. "What was it?"

"I don't know. I wish I did, but I don't."

"I searched the knight and found nothing," Kade admitted.

Ralf's eyebrows rose in shock. "You searched him?"

Kade nodded. "Unless the treasure was a chainmail tunic or some old worn boots, the knight had nothing on him."

"There was nothing?" Ralf frowned as his brother shook his head at his question. "I don't think that's going to stop Father. He's determined to find it. He's convinced the old knight had knowledge of a great Templar treasure." Ralf put a hand on Kade's shoulder. "He'll stop at nothing to find it. Perhaps you should leave again."

Kade met his brother's gaze. Both knew of their father's fury. Ralf's bruised eye was just the most recent evidence of it. It had been five years ago that Kade had left the castle and his family, unable to tolerate his father's brutality. He hadn't been strong enough in spirit or strength to face his father then. And his selfish, cowardly behavior had been eating away at him for the last five years. He had known the lashings and beatings would fall to Ralf. For that, he would be eternally sorry. "I'm not leaving again, Ralf. Not this time."

"He'll level the town to find his treasure."

Prickles of anxiety shot up Kade's spine. He immediately thought of Lia. He turned to look at her, but she had disappeared. His father would start with Lia because she had found the knight. Kade had to warn her. He glanced up and down the street.

"Kade, did you hear me?" Ralf called. "You have to leave. You buried the knight. Father will want to speak with you."

Kade didn't care. He nodded to Ralf, moving down the road. "Go and get your body. I still have time. If I leave, it will be an admission of guilt. I'm not going anywhere."

"Damn it, Kade," Ralf ground out, racing after him. Ralf grabbed his shoulder, halting his

Laurel O'Donnell

movement. "I'm his favorite and look what he does to me. Once Father learns you buried the knight, he'll be after you."

"Give me time. Throw him off my trail. Tell him whoever stabbed de Rolleston probably took the treasure. And it could be true."

"Where are you going?"

Kade didn't answer. He had to find Lia. She was in as much danger as he was.

CHAPTER FIVE

$\mathfrak{L}$ia entered the small chapel. There were enough wooden chairs to seat the entire village, the seats filling up nearly all the space in the small room. An aisle between the chairs stretched from the back of the chapel to the altar. The ceiling rose high over her head. She moved toward the altar at the front of the church. "Father?"

A balding man in a long brown robe lifted his head from his bent position at the side wall. He held a cloth in his hand. "Lia!"

As he pushed himself to his feet, Lia moved to his side joyfully. She embraced Father Stephen. "It's so good to see you."

"And you, child."

She glanced at the cloth in his hand.

"One of the children got sick at mass this morning," Father Stephen said.

"Do you need help?"

"I think that's all," Father Stephen said, inspecting the stone floor. "The poor boy." He looked at her with his kind blue eyes. "Poor little James. Perchance you could visit him and bring him something for his stomach."

Lia nodded. "I will." They both knew that James's mother would not let Lia give her anything to help James. She thought what she and Maeve did with their herbs was witchcraft and would not accept anything from her or Maeve. But Lia would try because she gave Father Stephen her word.

"What brings you into town?"

Lia hesitated, glancing at the door in the back of the chapel. She reached into her chemise and pulled out the parchment. "I was hoping you could read this for me."

Father Stephen took the parchment and scanned it. "What is this?" He became quiet as he looked the parchment over, reading its contents. He scowled fiercely. "Where did you get this?" There was something accusatory in the tone of his voice.

"I was given it," Lia said defensively. When Father Stephen looked at her, she added, "What does it say?"

Father Stephen shook his head and lowered his gaze to the parchment. "It was the knight, wasn't it? He gave it to you."

"What does it say?"

Father Stephen's frown deepened, etching thick lines in his forehead. "This is dangerous, Lia," he whispered. "Let me keep it."

"No," she said, almost panicking. Her heart beat faster. She had promised the knight she would protect it. "He gave it to me to keep safe. It's my responsibility."

"Lia..." He looked at her, leaning in and whispering. "It's too much responsibility for you. He shouldn't have asked you. You're just a child."

Insulted, Lia reached out and gently, but firmly, took it from him. "If you can't read it, I'll find someone who can."

"You jeopardize the life of every person you ask. Keep it hidden. Don't let anyone know you have it."

Lia looked down at the parchment. What was written on it that was so dangerous? That people could die over? "What does it say?"

"It is best if you don't know. Although, I doubt that will save your life."

Shocked, Lia snapped her gaze to Father Stephen. Troubled, frightened, Lia tucked the parchment into her chemise and backed up a step.

Father Stephen reached out and grasped her arm. "Keep it hidden," he warned.

"Keep what hidden?"

They turned to find Kade entering the chapel.

Anxiety shot through Lia. The Templar Knight and now Father Stephen had both warned her to keep the parchment hidden, but neither had told her what it said. Curiosity and trepidation burned inside her. Indecision plagued her.

"A kitten Lia found," Father Stephen finally answered. "From those two ruffians, Bors and Elias."

Kade stared at Lia as he approached. She averted her eyes.

"They are not kind to animals smaller than they are," Father Stephen added, removing his hand from her arm.

"Yes," Lia agreed. That was true, those two were always acting cruel to animals. "Thank you, Father."

He nodded, and she turned to Kade. His brow was etched in concern.

"You have to leave," Kade said.

She glanced back at Father Stephen strolling back to the altar before looking at Kade. "I was just leaving. James needs some basil and apples for his stomach –"

"No. I mean leave. Leave the village."

"Leave?" The thought was inconceivable. She had grown up here. Why would she leave the village? This was her home. Maeve was here. Her eyes widened as a horrible thought occurred to her. "Maeve. Is something wrong with Maeve?"

"Lia," Kade said firmly. "My father is looking for something that Sir de Rolleston, that knight, had. He's going to want to talk to you."

The parchment. He must be searching for the parchment. Ice shot down Lia's spine and dread filled her. She had seen what had happened to lady de Claremont.

Kade grasped her wrist. "I won't let that happen. He's not going to hurt you."

She looked into his sincere blue eyes and, maybe because she knew his mother, maybe because she wanted to, but she trusted him. He knew what his father was capable of. Even though she wanted to trust him, she still hesitated. "I don't know anything."

"He won't take that as an answer. You found the knight. Did you find anything on him?"

"No." She shook her head. Lord de Claremont wanted to speak to her. She recalled the bruises and cuts on lady de Claremont's face, as well as peppered over her body. If he had harmed his wife like that, what would he do to a peasant like her? Where was she to go? What would she do? How could she hide from such a powerful lord? This village was the only home she had ever known, these people the only ones she had ever known. "What about Maeve?"

"My father doesn't want her. He'll want you."

Her mind whirled, stunned. Leave Maeve? The thought was numbing. "No," she whispered, afraid. She pulled away from him. "I can't leave."

"You know what my father did to my mother. There were never any accidents, nor falls. He hit her. And he'll do worse to you." He squeezed her wrist. "You are not safe here. I can take you and Maeve to another village and you can start over. Somewhere where the bailiff doesn't know you. Somewhere my father can't find you."

Lia shook her head. "Maeve can't leave. She's too old."

"Then you must go."

Chills and fear engulfed her. She took a deep breath. "I won't leave her."

Frustration turned Kade's eyes dark and he released his hold on her. He shook his head, running his hand through his dark hair.

"I won't leave Maeve," Lia vowed.

Kade stared at Lia. Her brow was furrowed in anguish, her full lips turned down in a pout. And strands of that riotous red hair poked out from the braid like small flames, dancing about her shoulders in a gentle breeze. Lia wouldn't abandon Maeve. She wouldn't leave the woman she knew as a mother. Kade admired her and hated her in the same moment. She was doing what he couldn't. She was making the choice he wished he had made.

"Then we have to find the treasure my father is searching for. If we give it to him, he will leave you alone."

"Treasure?"

Kade nodded. "It was part of the Templar treasure. I'm not sure what it is, but my father is convinced Sir de Rolleston had something." He turned to leave the chapel.

Lia hurried after him, catching his arm and turning him. "Why are you doing this? Why help me?"

Kade's gaze moved over her face slowly as if savoring her. She was beautiful. But it was more than that. She was brave and protective, all the things he was not. She was caring and compassionate. "You helped my mother."

Lia's gaze softened, and she nodded, releasing him.

Kade turned away from her and moved out of the chapel. He realized he couldn't save his mother, but he could save Lia. Maybe somehow, someway, that would atone for his abandonment.

They walked down the road. Kade's mind began to work on the treasure. "I searched the knight. There was no treasure on him."

Lia walked beside him. "A ring? A pendant?"

Kade shook his head. "I must have missed it." He paused to glance back at the chapel. A group of soldiers stood in the graveyard near the church with Father Stephen, digging up Sir de Rolleston's freshly buried grave. He had searched de Rolleston's body quickly. Maybe too quickly. Would his father find the treasure?

"Maybe it wasn't treasure," Lia said.

Kade swiveled his gaze to her.

"I have a confession to make." Lia glanced at the soldiers and Father Stephen in the graveyard. She looked back at Kade and stepped closer to him as if to tell him a secret. "The knight was alive when I found him."

Kade tried desperately not to smile. He knew that already. But it was a start. At least she was beginning to trust him. He glanced down at the top of her dress where the dots of blood were. "He was wounded."

She nodded as her eyes widened in surprise. "Yes. I wanted to treat him, to help him. But he wouldn't even let me bring him back to Maeve." She lowered her remorseful gaze and a lock of her hair fell forward.

Kade caught it, and when she looked up at him he tucked it behind her ear. "I'm sure he knew he couldn't be saved."

"He should have let me try."

Kade watched the way her lips formed the words. So lovely, so… He mentally shook himself. He had to focus to save her. "He gave the treasure to you."

She began to shake her head, to deny it, but then stopped with a sigh. "I've been warned numerous times that it was dangerous. That I should tell no one that I have it."

She *did* have it! "Whatever that knight gave you is dangerous. Give it to me. I can stop this. I'll give it to my father and he won't look for it. You'll be safe."

Lia was silent for a long moment, weighing her options. She scowled fiercely and turned, walking down the road. "It's my responsibility." She stopped suddenly, and he almost ran into her. "I'm only telling you this because you offered to help me. I don't know what to do with it."

"Give it to me."

She shook her head again. "He gave it to me to keep safe."

"He gave it to you because you were the only one around. He didn't want it falling into the wrong hands."

"Your father's."

Kade nodded. "It seems that way."

Lia was silent again, considering. "I don't want anyone hurt because of it. How do I know if you give it to your father that more people won't be harmed?"

"What did he give you?"

She hesitated. "What if I tell you and you are in danger because of it?" She shook her head. "I couldn't live with myself. I couldn't do that."

He wanted to embrace her and hold her and kiss her for her concern. She was amazing. And the fact that she was worried over him made him desire her all the more. "How do you think I would feel if you were harmed, if my father hurt you to find this treasure. Please, Lia. Give it to me."

She shook her head. "I'll destroy it."

Kade looked at her in sympathy. "It won't stop my father. He will take his wrath out on everyone you love, everyone who helped you. The bailiff, the innkeeper, those two young men. Even Maeve. And then you."

Lia was silent for a long moment. "If I go away with you, will the others be safe?"

Kade felt a welling of warmth expand from his heart through his body. She would sacrifice herself for the ones she loved. For Maeve, the innkeeper, for the village. He admired her. She was frightened and afraid, but so brave. "We can make sure Father knows you have the treasure. He'll leave them alone and come after you."

"I have to say goodbye to Maeve." She stared at the chapel and the soldiers working to dig up the grave. Her voice was thick and heavy. "Then I'll go with you."

CHAPTER SIX

$\mathbb{L}$ia quietly helped Maeve with the evening meal, chopping the vegetables to put in the stew. Her heart was heavy, her sadness all consuming. She didn't want to leave Maeve. Maeve had raised her, had always been kind to her, and she loved her as if she were her own mother. She would protect Maeve any way she had to. When she saw those soldiers digging up the Templar knight's grave, she knew she had to leave. The situation was far more serious than she could have imagined. For men to dig up a corpse in pursuit of some believed treasure was sacrilegious. What words could possibly be on the parchment to cause this much chaos and death? Why did Kade's father want that parchment with such desperate urgency?

Maeve sat beside her, her weathered face looking concerned. "You are quiet, child."

Lia frowned, moving her wrist to slice the knife through the carrot.

Maeve placed a hand over hers, stilling her movement. "It doesn't matter what others think. You must do your own thinking."

Lia looked at Maeve. She had thought about the parchment over and over, about what it held for her future. She couldn't decipher any other way out. She didn't know what to do. She wanted to confide in Maeve, but she knew that knowledge would only put her in danger.

"James's mother does not want our help and we must accept that. The boy will recover," Maeve said.

James, the child with the stomach ache. Lia felt a bit of the tenseness leave her shoulders. Of course, that would be what Maeve was speaking about. Lia dropped her gaze to the sliced carrot.

"Or are you thinking of that young lord?"

Lia's gaze snapped to Maeve's. Was she speaking of Kade? How did she know?

"Many saw the two of you speaking in the village. He is handsome, is he not?" Maeve smiled her gummy grin.

Lia felt a heated blush of warmth spread over her cheeks. Yes, he was indeed handsome, but he would never think of her that way.

"There is nothing to be ashamed of. You are a beautiful girl."

Beautiful was not a way people described her. Her red hair lent many of the villagers to believe she was a spawn of the devil, or a witch. Beautiful was not a description they used for her. And then she thought of a way to make this believable, thinking of a way to use this gossip to make what she needed to tell Maeve make sense to the old woman. She sat in the chair. "Yes, we were talking."

Maeve patted her hand, patiently.

"And he is handsome. Very handsome." Lia was startled at the truth in her statement. When she pictured Kade, his deep blue eyes, his confident stature, the way his grin sent warmth through her body, she realized exactly how handsome he was. She stared at the chopped carrots on the wooden table without really seeing them.

Maeve grinned. "He seems nice."

Lia had to look away before Maeve saw the lie in her eyes. "I love him." She was surprised at how easy the words came to her.

Maeve sat back. "Oh, child."

"He is kind to me and says he loves me. He wants to take me away. He said he will keep me safe."

"You are safe here."

Guilt settled heavily in Lia's stomach like a large rock. She wished she could tell Maeve the truth. That she was leaving to protect her, that she could think of no other way. She grasped Maeve's hands tightly. "Maeve, I would do anything for you, you know that."

Maeve nodded. "Love is powerful, child. But it is dangerous. It blinds us to darker things. Are you sure he is who you think he is?"

Lia nodded. "Yes. I'm certain.

Maeve tried to peer deeper into her eyes. "Are you certain?"

Lia nodded her head again, but couldn't meet Maeve's eyes. "Yes." Her chest tightened. How she wished she didn't have to leave with a lie between them. "He said he has enough coin for a cruck. We can live there and raise a family."

"Lia," Maeve said softly. "He is a lord. He must marry a lady. He will keep you in the cruck until he tires of you."

Her throat closed, and tears filled her eyes at her uncertain future. She rose to her feet. "How can you say that? He loves me!" No. No. No. This was not the way she wanted to leave. She took a deep breath. "I have to do this, Maeve. I'm sorry." She hurried to the door and paused to chance a glance back at Maeve. Her mother, for all sakes and purposes, sat in the chair looking so much older than she had ever seen her. Her shoulders were hunched; her gray hair had come free of the knot at the top of her hair and strings hung down around her face.

Lia's heart ached, and she raced to Maeve's side, dropping to her knees. "Please Maeve. I'll be fine. Kade will protect me." She wrapped her arms around her waist. "I love you and could never, never repay all you've done for me."

Maeve stroked her hair. "I've done nothing but love you."

The tears rushed to Lia's eyes. Her very soul cried out. Of everyone in the entire world, she loved Maeve so. That was why she had to leave. "Please, Maeve. Let me go," she whispered into Maeve's cotton smock, her voice catching on the lump in her throat.

"Of course," she whispered soothingly. "I can't hold you here."

Lia rose and moved to the door, wiping a hand across her nose.

"Take care, child," Maeve whispered through a thick voice.

Lia hurried from the cruck, sobs welling inside of her.

Kade waited outside the cruck. It was dark when Lia emerged. Her eyes were swollen with sorrow; tears ringed them with sadness. He felt her agony and instinctively opened his arms to her. She fell into them, her entire body racked with weeping.

He silently held her, rubbing her back, stroking her hair. He rested his cheek against the top of her head, squeezing his eyes closed. He wished she had never become involved in this. He wished she could have gone on living her life in quiet harmony. "I'm sorry," he said softly.

Lia shook her head and stepped back from him, wiping her cheeks. "It has to be this way," she said firmly. "There's only one thing I want to know." She reached inside her dress and pulled out the piece of parchment, presenting it to Kade. "What does it say?"

Kade stared at the parchment gripped in her fingers. For a moment, he was confused. He eased the parchment from her hand. It was old, crinkling in his grip. He stared at the folded parchment and then looked at Lia.

Her eyes were red from crying, her lashes clumped together, her cheeks lined with the path of her tears.

"I have to know what is so important, what's worth life and death."

Understanding dawned in Kade as he looked back at the parchment. He was startled it was so simple. Just a piece of parchment. Not really a treasure at all. What had he been expecting? Diamonds? Jewels? Incredible wealth? Gold beyond reason? Maybe it was a map. He opened it. He stared at the words there, reading them. With each word he read, understanding slowly trickled into his disbelief, along with an incredible sense of doom. This was no simple treasure. This was something he could not even fathom. He reread the words. When he was finished, he knew they were in deep trouble for he knew with absolute certainty he could never give the parchment over to his father.

Lia watched Kade as he carefully read the parchment. She saw the transformation in his features. His furrowed brow slowly eased and rose in amazement. When he lifted his gaze to hers, there was wonder and trepidation in his stare.

"What does it say?" she demanded. She had to know. Even through all the danger and warnings, she had to know what was on the parchment, what was written there. What was so important that men were willing to kill to get it? What was so important that she had to leave her home, so Maeve would be safe?

"It's a list," Kade murmured, looking back at the parchment, then up at her.

"A list of Templar knights?" Lia asked, encouraging him to continue.

"You don't want to know this. It will only put you in more danger."

Shock raced through her. How many men had told her that? No, that was unacceptable. She snatched the parchment from his hands. "I deserve to know. For everything I'm giving up, I deserve to know!"

Kade sighed. "You're right. I'm sorry." He nodded. "It *is* a list of Templar knights. And their treasure. It lists what each knight has in his possession.

Lia looked at the jumble of strokes on the parchment, her brow furrowing. "It must be a lot of coin."

"None of it is coin. Look." He eased the parchment from her fingers and flattened it against his hand. He pointed to a line. "Here. This knight has the crown of thorns from Jesus's head." He pointed to another line. "This knight has a ring with God's name on it. And here." He shifted to the last line. "The ark of the covenant."

Like a curtain being drawn aside to reveal the sun, the powerful knowledge of what the parchment held was revealed to her. "This can't be real."

"I think it is."

Lia stared at the black lines on the parchment. Suddenly, the danger was real. The information was deadly. Men would kill to possess these items and their rumored power.

"And my father will think it is real. He will want to get his hands on these powerful relics." He looked at the parchment again, his brow furrowed in concentration. "I don't even know what some of these items are. If the Templars had them, I am sure they are important. My father can never get this list. He can't be allowed to know who has possession of these relics. He would hunt them all down, kill every knight to have this kind of power." Kade shook his head, running his hand through his dark hair.

Lia nodded. "That is why we are leaving."

"It's not enough. He will never stop looking for it." He took her hands into his, touched the side of her face. "I had hoped you might be able to live a normal life, starting over in a new village." He scowled. "But this…" He crumpled the parchment in his fist. "He will never stop looking for it."

A sinking feeling pulled her down, but it had nothing to do with the parchment. It was Maeve's words: 'He will keep you in the cruck until he tires of you.' She was under no illusions of what her life would be. But the thought that Kade would not be with her, made her feel lost and alone. She had assumed he would stay with her. How foolish she was. She didn't want to be alone. She wished she had never received that parchment. She wished she had never found that knight. "Burn it."

"What?"

"We should destroy it," she suggested.

Kade looked at the parchment in his fist thoughtfully. "And lose all those relics?"

"No. They would not be lost. They would be protected."

"Is that what de Rolleston would have done? He gave it to you instead of burning it. He died protecting it, but he didn't destroy it." Kade looked at the parchment again. "It's too valuable to destroy."

She sighed softly as she thought about the Templar knight. He had died alone. Was that her future? "That poor knight," she whispered.

Kade looked at her.

"Sir de Rolleston. He knew what he had. And he died defending it."

"He was a coward," Kade grumbled. "He should never have given it to you."

"He was dying. He could do nothing else. He knew he had to protect it. He couldn't keep it. Your father would have found it. He would have searched his body just like you did." She looked at him with suspicion, taking a step away from him. "Did you know about the list?"

Kade shook his head. "No!" He chuckled bitterly. "My father would never have given me that precious information."

"You don't get along with your father."

Kade grinned, but it was cold and humorless. "No."

It was strange how she had longed for a mother all her life and Kade had longed to be fatherless.

"I have an idea." Kade said as he began to move toward the forest where his horse was tethered.

Lia followed him. "Are you going to destroy it?"

"No."

Anxiety swirled through her. "Are you leaving me?"

Kade stopped and turned to her. His gaze moved over her, and he stepped toward her. "I'm trying to help you."

"I've given you the parchment," Lia mumbled. "It's what your father wants. And even though I was charged with protecting it, I haven't done such a good job." He took a step closer as she rambled. "I told Maeve I was leaving her. And I would to keep her safe. But now, you have the only thing that will protect her and –"

He pulled her against him. "I won't leave you."

His deep voice resonated through her with promise. His hold was warm and strong. She watched his lips form his words; the sensual way they moved. All she could think of was kissing his lips. Instead, she murmured, "What's your plan?"

He brushed a strand of red hair from her cheek. He cupped her face and eased his lips to hers. The strength of his lips set her body aflame. Instantly upon meeting his mouth with her own, her world tilted, and every worry evaporated. She felt her knees weaken as he explored her mouth, moving over every inch. She sighed against him, parting her lips for his exploration. And he did explore her. He thrust his tongue forward, sweeping it into her mouth. She pulled him closer, his entire body flush against the length of hers.

He eased his head from hers, groaning softly. "I wish we had more time," he whispered and stepped back.

She instinctively reached for him as the chilled air filled the space where he had been.

He untethered the reins of his horse from the tree branch and mounted. He moved his horse in a circle around her before heading off toward town.

Lia watched him disappear, his kiss still wet on her lips. She touched her swollen lips; her heart beat with aching. And then she remembered he had not answered her question.

A KNIGHT'S PROTECTION

Kade leaned against the chapel doorframe. He watched the setting sun, the direction he knew Lia was. He hated leaving her alone. He kept thinking of how alone his mother had been in her final hours. He pushed the thought from his mind.

This would keep Lia safe. He was doing this for her.

"You wanted to see me," a voice called from inside the chapel.

He knew his brother had been in the village and had sent a boy to give him a message. Now, as he turned to face him, Kade felt victorious. He finally felt they had the upper hand against their father. He grinned at Ralf.

Ralf narrowed his eyes. "Are you still keeping company with that witch?" There was disgust in his voice.

"Witch?" Kade repeated, confused.

"The herbalist's little red-headed helper."

"Lia? Yes. She is helping me." Confusion washed over Kade.

"Be careful how she helps you. She helped Mother, too."

Kade nodded solemnly. "I know. I'm grateful she was there."

"Grateful?" Ralf asked, his lips twisting in shocked disbelief.

Kade nodded. "She soothed her. She stayed with her in her final moments. She was a help and comfort to Mother."

Ralf laughed viciously. "Is that what she told you?"

"Yes," Kade admitted. "She said –"

"She killed Mother!"

"What?" Kade asked, stunned. He couldn't believe it. Lia would never... "Be certain what you say, brother," he said quietly, dangerously.

"I was there. I saw what she did. You weren't. Mother was getting better before each of the little witch's visits. When she left..." Ralf shook his head. "...she would be in agony."

Kade remembered Lia telling him the same thing. He shook his head. "She would never hurt Mother."

Ralf nodded in understanding. "She's put you under her spell. Just like she did to Mother."

"No. Lia tries to help. She –"

"You weren't there. Mother got worse after her visits!"

Still, Kade refused to believe Lia would harm his mother. "Why? Why would she do that?"

Ralf shrugged. "All I know is what happened. Every day, Mother called for her. Every day. She begged me to bring the little witch to her. I did. And when she left, Mother was worse."

"Didn't you watch what she did? Did you leave Mother alone with her?"

Ralf waved his hand. "I didn't know what she was mixing, what she gave Mother. And Father didn't care. He ordered me to bring her to Mother, so Mother would shut up."

"Why would Lia hurt Mother? She is a healer."

Ralf shrugged. "I would escort her to the door of the keep after her visits and by the time I returned to Mother's side, she was bent over in pain."

Kade scowled. It didn't make sense. Lia told him she sat with his mother and talked to her. She said she tried to ease her pain. She even gave him a message from Mother. Why would Lia give her anything to cause her pain?

"I don't care if you believe me or not. I'm just warning you."

Kade was too confused to answer Ralf. He couldn't picture kind, beautiful Lia poisoning his mother. She tried to help everyone. Why would she poison Mother?

Ralf looked up at the wooden cross on the altar. "What do you want, Kade?" Ralf demanded. "Why did you send for me?"

Kade looked up at his brother. He was going to tell him about the treasure, about the parchment. Now, the treasure didn't seem important. "You're sure about Lia?"

"I can only tell you what I saw." He sighed softly. "Who are you going to believe? Your brother or a murdering witch?"

Kade ground his teeth. She lied! Lia had lied to him. Now, he even wondered if her message from his mother was true. "Father can't find the treasure?"

Ralf paused half way down the aisle. "He will, in time. He has too many men out looking for it." Ralf stopped suddenly and whirled on him. "You found it. That's why you sent for me."

Kade ground his teeth, anger rising inside of him. Lia had poisoned his mother? "Are you certain?"

"Certain? Certain about you finding the treasure?"

"About Lia hurting Mother."

Ralf stiffened, insulted. "I told you what I saw. Did you find the treasure?"

Fury washed over him. His brother had seen Lia give his mother something, something that caused her pain. "Yes. I found it," he growled. He pulled the parchment from his tunic.

"You won. You beat Father. You found the knight first. You found the treasure first."

"It doesn't matter that I beat Father." Nothing really mattered except that Lia had killed his mother, hurt her, and let her die in pain. She had lied to him, deceived him.

Ralf approached Kade. "What is it? What does it say?"

Kade handed him the parchment.

Ralf scanned it and his smooth brow furrowed as he read it. "No wonder Father wants this list." He lifted joyful eyes to Kade. "Do you know what this means? We have power now. We can use this to get him to stop hurting us. I can finally become lord of Castle de Claremont."

Kade didn't care. His mind swirled. Lia hurt his mother. She had killed her! He gritted his teeth, setting his jaw tight. How gullible he was for believing her.

Ralf grabbed Kade's tunic in a fist. "We have something he wants, Kade. We can negotiate. He can have the damned parchment, if he makes me lord. We'll finally be free of him. He can spend the rest of his life searching for the knights and their treasure. I don't give a damn. As long as he leaves us alone." Ralf pulled Kade into a tight hug.

But Kade didn't feel victorious. Anger simmered through his veins.

CHAPTER SEVEN

The sun had set a long time ago. Lia wore a path in the leaves and dirt of the forest floor, awaiting Kade's return. She hid herself in the trees, not far from the road. The moon rose, a mocking sliver of an eye, gazing at her through the leaves of the swaying trees.

Where was he? She stopped and looked toward the village again. She should go after him, but she didn't know where he had gone. And he had the parchment! Oh, how silly she had been to give it to him. It was her responsibility!

She shook her head. She trusted Kade. She would not doubt him.

The sound of a horse's hooves echoed in the distance, drawing closer. Was it Kade? She took a step from the cover of the trees. Had he come back? Realization struck her too late. It wasn't the sound of one horse, but many.

A group of men on horseback emerged from the forest, closing in.

Lia stepped back.

They brought their horses to a halt when they spotted her. She scanned the men and recognized Kade. Relief swept through her. "Kade!" She moved toward him.

Two men dismounted and intercepted her, taking hold of her arms to hold her back.

Kade's eyes blazed blue fire as he stared at her. There was a coldness to him she didn't recognize.

"Kade," she called.

His brother signaled the men with a wave of his hand. "Take her to the castle."

"Kade," she whispered. Was he pretending? Was this part of his plan? She felt the terror grow inside her. He was not pretending. She had experienced rejection and hate for her entire life and she knew his gaze was real.

Her arms were jerked back behind her and secured with a rope.

She couldn't stop looking at him. His lips were thinned, his eyes hard. His fingers clenched the reins of the horse so hard his knuckles turned white.

One of the guards lifted her onto a horse and mounted behind her.

"What have I done?" she whispered to herself as much as him.

"You killed my mother," Kade snarled.

Lia's mouth dropped open in shock.

Ralf urged his steed up beside her. "You will be hung as the witch you are."

Her world crumbled around her. It felt as though she were falling. Not because of the proclamation from the brother, but because of Kade's betrayal. She closed her mouth, fighting back the tears that threatened. She dropped her chin in defeat as the horses started down the road, toward the castle.

Kade watched the squad of soldiers and his brother move down the road. Lia had not denied the accusation. She had simply looked at him with such anguish and hurt that he felt the breath rush from his lungs. His horse tossed his head as if in accusation. Kade turned the horse in a circle to steady him and noticed the cruck. The old woman stood in the doorway, locks of her scraggly hair and her thin figure accented by a fire burning inside the cruck behind her.

Kade moved his horse forward. He wasn't sure why he approached, or what he would say to her. He was only hoping for answers. "You visited the castle with Lia to tend my mother?" he asked as he reached the old woman.

Maeve nodded. "On occasion. Lia went without me at times. I think your mother enjoyed her company. They were closer in age. She was lonely, I think, after you left."

This wounded Kade. He and his mother had always been close. Then he became angry at his father's vile behavior and that rage had blinded him to everyone around him, including his mother. He frowned at the old woman's words. Why would his mother befriend Lia? Of all the people in the village, of all the people in the castle, why Lia? He knew this answer, he realized. He had befriended Lia too, had fallen under her charm. "You and Lia know a lot about herbs. Are there herbs that can kill?"

"Of course. You know that. Everyone knows that."

"Has Lia ever used them?"

"You'll have to ask Lia that."

His horse whinnied and Kade tightened his grip. "Why would Lia want to kill my mother?"

A long silence ensued before she answered, "That is a question for Lia."

Kade didn't like these answers. They settled nothing. He scowled at the woman, then turned his horse toward the road.

"She was willing to go away with you," Maeve said, calling after him. "She trusted you enough to see to her safety."

Kade turned back to the old woman. "I didn't know what I know now."

"She has faith in you. She loves you."

Her statement startled him. She couldn't love him. He scowled fiercely. "She murdered my mother!"

Maeve was silent for a long moment, staring at him. There was something gentle and compassionate in her gaze that made Kade feel guilty. And he shouldn't feel guilty! "My brother told me! He saw it."

"Did he? Perhaps you should be questioning what he saw."

Frustrated by her vague answers and the doubt she put in his mind, Kade turned away and spurred his horse down the road.

She loves you. The old woman's words echoed in his mind. Love. How could she love him?

Kade shook his head, his hand clenching the mug he held. Love him. But that wasn't what bothered him the most. He had betrayed her trust. She had given him the parchment and he had handed her over to his brother. She deserves it, he told himself. He sat in the Great Hall, unable to relax, even with the amount of ale he had already drunk. The Hall was empty; a low fire burned in the hearth. Servants slept close to the hearth for warmth.

Ralf had seen her do it. He said she had poisoned their mother. Kade frowned and wondered why he didn't entirely believe his own brother.

Still, Kade couldn't get rid of this doubt that nagged at him about Lia. There was no reason for her to kill his mother. None. She was gentle and kind. Killing, poisoning, wasn't in her nature. Or was it? Kade grimaced. He stood quickly, knocking over the chair. He had to have answers! Why? Why would she do it? Why kill his mother? He stormed out of the Great Hall.

He followed the corridor and entered a door. Stairs led down to the dungeon; he took them two at a time. He was angry at being deceived. He had befriended her! He had trusted her. He had…admired her. He slowed when he saw the two guards standing before the long hallway of cells in the dungeon. "Which one is she in?"

"Second one on this side, m'lord," one of the guards said.

Kade moved by them to the cell. He slid the bolt on the door aside and threw it open. The flickering light from the torch on the wall cut through the darkness to illuminate Lia. She sat on the floor of the dungeon cell, her knees pulled up to her chest, her red hair wild about her head. She looked up and he saw two pools of blue shimmering in the torchlight. His heart twisted instinctively. This unexpected, unwanted feeling made him even more angry. "Why did you do it?"

She bowed her head.

He stomped into the cell. "Why did you kill my mother?"

"Where's the parchment?" Her voice was small, but ferocious.

"I gave it to my brother."

She flinched as if he had struck her. Her face came up and there was anger glimmering in her eyes. "I trusted you."

"And I believed you."

"He'll give it to your father. You were the one that said your father could never get it."

"We are family. He will never give it to Father."

"You said it yourself. You are family. He will not betray your father."

Dark, molten fury burned through his veins at her words. His fists clenched. "Are you saying my brother would betray me?"

"He already has."

Lies and more lies. He shook his head. "He's my brother. He told me what happened with mother."

"I told you what happened with your mother."

"What did you use to kill her with? What herb?"

Lia shook her head and looked down again. "You wouldn't believe me if I told you."

"Tell me!" Kade demanded.

Lia looked up at him again. "I would have done it. Lady de Claremont begged me to end her life every day I went to see her. Just something to put her to sleep. Just something to make the pain go away forever. Nothing I gave her was enough to stop what your father was doing to her."

Kade's eyes widened. She knew there were no accidents. She knew his mother was not clumsy.

"The beatings were horrible. I would come back the next day and there would be new bruises on her stomach and back." Lia shook her head. "I gave her everything I could think of to ease her pain. But it wasn't enough. She was broken, in body as well as spirit."

The image she painted was gruesome. His mother slipping away beneath his father's lashings.

"The one thing I couldn't figure out was your brother. He must have known. If he didn't hear or see the beatings, he must have seen the bruises on her face, on her arms. She had different bruises each day. He never said a word to me about what was happening. He never spoke to me."

Kade scowled and half turned away from her in embarrassment. She had tried to help his mother. He had known it all along. "You didn't kill my mother." He had abandoned his mother. And now, he had abandoned Lia in his disbelief.

"I was afraid. I was horrified she would even ask me to end her life. I was a coward for not doing it."

"No," he said firmly. "Not a coward. A saint. An angel for watching her go through that, for standing beside her."

"I couldn't stop it. I couldn't stop the abuse. I couldn't stop the pain. I did nothing."

Kade dropped to his knees before her. "You did more than I could... Than I *did* do."

"And yet, it wasn't enough for you to believe in me." She looked down at her bound hands. "It wasn't enough to save her...or me."

"Because it is easier to believe people are evil." He took her hands, her soft hands, into his own. "It was easier for me to believe you were bad. That you would take my mother's life instead of try to save it." She tried to pull her hands free, but he held them tight. "Because I was raised with evil. I was raised to think all people were like that. Until I met you, I thought it was true. I thought there was no way to stop my father. But I was wrong. It was my job to save my mother. But instead, I left. I left her to my father." Lia's hands tightened around his own. Even after his betrayal, she still sought to comfort him. "I won't do the same with you."

He leaned his forehead against hers. "I love you, Lia," he whispered.

Lia lifted her hands to frame his face. She lifted her lips to his, brushing them against his.

"I'm sorry," he whispered into her kiss.

She shook her head as the kiss deepened. Tingles of life danced across his skin, heating his body, waking his soul.

"Your father can't get the parchment. Don't let him. No matter what happens to me," Lia whispered.

"Nothing is going to happen to you." Kade rose. "But you must remain here for a little while longer. I will come for you by morning." He turned toward the door with purpose.

"Kade!"

He stopped and turned to her.

"I didn't want to tell you about your mother. I didn't want you to think of her like that. In that much pain."

Lord, he loved her. She was protecting him! She had always been protecting him. "I'm glad you did."

Kade strolled down the hall. He knew Lia was safe for the time being, even though he couldn't stand thinking of her in that rotting dungeon. He had to make things right with her. He had been wrong giving the parchment to Ralf. Even to save them, his father could never get it. He would never hand over that much power to him.

He took the stairs of the spiral stairway toward the family bed chambers. As he reached the second floor, he saw Ralf coming down the hall toward him.

"There you are," Ralf greeted. "Father wants to speak to you."

Kade nodded. "Do you have the parchment?" He waited for his brother to reach him. Ralf nodded his head and patted his belt. "Let me see it." He held out his hand.

Ralf hesitated for a moment. Then, he reached down to his belt and pulled the parchment out. He handed it to Kade.

Kade opened it and scanned it. "Are you certain we should give this to him?"

"Of course!" Ralf exclaimed. "He'll go on his treasure hunt and give me control of the castle. We'll be free of him!"

Kade looked at the parchment again. "The Ark of the Covenant? Imagine if he gets these items. The power he would have. It's too much power for one man."

"You don't believe this is real, do you?"

"Yes. I do. A Templar knight died defending this from father." His voice softened, and he turned away from Ralf. "Mother died arguing with father about it."

"Mother didn't know about the treasure!"

Kade whirled back to him. "Maybe she did and she was trying to protect it."

Ralf stared at Kade in disbelief. He shook his head. "We can be free, Kade. Do you know what that means?"

"But at what cost?"

Ralf snatched the parchment from Kade's fingers. "At any cost. I've put up with enough from Father. You left. It's my turn to be free now."

Stunned, Kade could only watch his brother walk down the hallway toward his father's chambers. The bitterness and anger in Ralf's voice shocked Kade. He had never realized how disappointed his brother was with him, how resentful Ralf was that he left him. Tingles danced along the nape of Kade's neck, a warning. He glanced back down the hallway toward the stairs and Lia. He should get her and leave. Run. Escape.

But, the parchment... The treasure. His mother's warning. He couldn't let Lia down. He had to make sure his father didn't get it. He quickly followed Ralf toward his father's chambers.

Ralf had knocked and was opening the door when Kade reached him. They entered together. The room was dark, cold. Just like his father. Kade had often been called into his father's room for discipline and the memories of those unpleasant meetings sent a chill through his body.

The hearth was lit, casting flickering shadows over the room. A large bed sat against one wall, covered in thick darkness. His father sat in the middle of the bed, looking weak and feeble. "Where is my treasure?" his father demanded.

Kade looked at Ralf for a moment. "We have it."

A bony hand stretched out from the confines of his father's nightshirt. "Give it to me."

Ralf stepped forward. Kade laid a hand on his chest. "We have some demands before we hand it over."

"Demands?" his father asked in disgust. He began to sputter, half coughing, half laughing. He stopped suddenly. "Ralf. Give it to me."

Ralf stepped forward, his hand outstretched with the parchment in his fist.

Kade snatched the parchment. "I said we had some requirements before we hand this over."

The silence that spread through the room was thick and oppressing.

"Just like your mother," his father said softly. "She thought she could control me, too. You've always been like her. Not nearly far sighted enough."

"You only want this parchment and what is on it. We mean nothing to you. Mother meant nothing to you."

His father's mouth twisted. "Fear and power are the only truth in the world. That parchment holds power."

"And I hold the parchment."

More silence. Kade could see Ralf where he stood before the hearth. He didn't understand why his brother didn't demand what was his, why he didn't stand up to his father. He was the one that came up with the plan.

"Are you going to stand there all day or are you going to tell me what you want?" his father demanded.

Kade took a breath. "You will never lay a hand on either of us again." His father chuckled, but Kade hurried to continue, "And you will step aside as Lord of de Claremont and allow Ralf to take his rightful seat."

More silence stretched through the room. The flames flickered and cracked behind him.

"You can go chase your treasure, but leave the castle to Ralf," Kade clarified.

His father grimaced. His gaze shifted from Kade to Ralf. "Him? Lord? He can't even utter a word to me. What kind of lord will he make?"

"He'll make a fine lord. A fair lord. A generous lord who cares about his people," Kade defended, his hand fisting around the parchment.

"A weak lord. Is this what you want, boy? To take my title from me? To become lord?"

The silence became heavy, making Kade uneasy. He shifted to look at Ralf. Indecision lined Ralf's brow. They locked gazes for a moment before Ralf dropped his.

"No, Father," he whispered.

"Speak up, boy!" his father snapped.

Ralf shook his head. "No, Father. It's not what I want."

"Ralf," Kade pleaded.

But it was too late. Desperation filled Kade. He should have known, known what Ralf was going to do. His brother was not as strong as he was. He couldn't defy his father, not after years of being under his mistreatment and tyranny. Kade had abandoned him and now Ralf abandoned Kade, siding with his father. In doing so, he had sealed his fate.

"You left," Ralf whispered. "I was alone."

His father chuckled, the horrible cackling sound filling the room. "Give me the parchment and I will let you and that little slut you've been with leave the castle alive and unharmed."

Kade looked at Ralf. "What about Ralf?"

"What about him? He is heir and will remain with me."

Ralf looked up at Kade and there was such anguish and fear in his eyes that desperation fisted around Kade's heart. He had left his mother and Ralf alone with a monster. His mother was dead, but his brother wasn't. Kade shook his head. He thrust the parchment toward the hearth. "No. I won't leave him. If you want this parchment, the power and fear it holds, the treasure, you will make Ralf lord."

"No!" his father called, reaching for the parchment, even though he was across the room from it. "Don't!"

Kade marveled at the fear in his father's eyes, the horror. "You're right on one account, father. This parchment does hold power."

His father sat back in the bed, his teeth clenching, twisting his lips into a grotesque snarl. "Fine. Fine. You want the castle, the lands, take them. He can be lord. Just give me the parchment."

"After you sign over the necessary paperwork, you can have it."

Lia clutched her knees. Her legs were pulled up to her chest as she sat with her head bent in the darkness of the dungeon. It was chilly, and damp and the constant drip drip drip of water was going to make her go mad.

Strangely, her mind wandered to Kade. He warmed her skin just by looking at her. The way he held her in his arms comforted her. How she wanted to be in those strong arms right now.

He said he loved her! Loved her! She had believed that love was beyond her reach. No one wanted to love an outcast. And she hadn't dared to hope that anyone would, no matter what Maeve told her.

But Kade had. He did. She was worried about him. And Maeve. She was worried that alone with his brother and father, Kade would forget he loved her. She shook her head against her knees. She couldn't think like that. She had to have faith in him. He was stronger than he thought.

Have faith, she told herself over and over. Because she did love him. She loved him so very much.

Suddenly, the cell door opened. Lia looked up hopefully, but had to look away when a bright torch was shoved into the dark cell.

Two armored guards came in. They grasped her arms and pulled her to her feet.

"Where's Kade?" she asked.

They didn't answer her, but pulled her from the cell, holding her tightly between them.

Fear engulfed Lia. She was being led to the courtyard where she would be burned as a witch. Kade had failed. "Where are you taking me?"

Her heart hammered in her chest. She could barely keep up with the pace the guards set as they walked down the dungeon corridor and then up the stairs with her. They turned down a long stone hallway. Torches lined the wall, casting circles of light in the dark tunnel.

They pulled her through a massive double door into a room that was so large she could fit ten of her crucks into it. Her gaze swept the room. Standing before the hearth she saw three men, and another man sat in a chair; they all looked at a large wooden table and what was on it.

Lia gasped as one of them looked up at her. Kade! She pulled her arms free of the guards and quickly moved toward him. He walked toward her, and they met halfway across the room. She stopped short before him, trying to read his expression, trying to decipher what had happened.

Kade reached forward and pulled her into his embrace. "It's all right," he whispered.

Relief swept through her and her knees almost buckled. She clutched him tightly.

"Give it to me now. I've done as you requested," the voice from the chair cackled.

Kade pulled back from Lia. He kept her hand captive in his and led her to the table.

Lia recognized his brother instantly. She assumed the man in the chair was his father. The other man, dressed in a fine, rich embroidered jupon, with his brown hair cut bowl length, she did not know.

"Give it to me," his father repeated, stretching his hand out toward Kade across the table.

Kade looked at the unknown man. "Is it all in order?"

"Aye. Lord Ralf will take control of the castle and lands."

Kade glanced at Ralf.

His father stretched out his hand further, greedily.

Kade turned to Lia. The look he bestowed on her was strange. She couldn't read the meaning behind it in the flickering light that fell over his face from the hearth. His hand tightened around hers. "One more thing, Father, before I do. I want the truth. What happened to mother?"

Impatience glittered in the old man's eyes. Red light reflected in them from the hearth. "Happened? She fell."

"The truth," Kade insisted. "Her final week. She was not getting better. She got worse. The bruises –"

He waved a slim hand. "Yes, yes. She was weak."

"And she called for her," Ralf accused, pointing at Lia. "That's what you said."

The grumbling cackle his father produced sent tremors down Lia's spine. "Her? No. She called for Kade. For you. Repeatedly. And I became tired of it. Of her."

Lia's hand tightened around Kade's in comfort. She stroked his arm to ease the pain he must be feeling.

"You killed her," Kade charged.

"I silenced her."

Kade's jaw clenched and looked at his brother. "Lia didn't kill mother. She helped her as best she could."

His brother knew the truth now. The truth that she and Kade had already known. She didn't kill his mother.

"Give it to me. You promised," his father said, stretching out his hand.

Kade yanked the parchment from his belt and handed it to his father.

Lia's mouth dropped open. "No," she whispered.

His father's old wrinkled face lit with triumph as he snatched the parchment from Kade's hold and peeled it open to gaze upon the written words. The treasure.

"No," Lia said more forcefully.

"Lia," Kade replied firmly.

She tried to pull her hand from his hold. "You told me your father could never have it. You told me it was too important."

Her father began to laugh. A high pitched joyful noise that echoed in the great room.

Lia struggled in Kade's tight hold. This was wrong! That parchment was hers! Tears stung her eyes.

Kade grabbed her shoulders, stilling her fight, and looked into her eyes. "This is for the best."

For the best? Her mind repeated. The best for whom? "I was supposed to protect it," she whispered. That knight had died protecting it and she had given it to Kade. She struck his cheek hard, the slap resounding throughout the room. He released her, and she stepped back.

The guards began to pull their swords from their sheaths, but Kade stilled them with a raised hand.

Lia's world blurred as tears filled her eyes. "I trusted you," she whispered, but in the silent room her accusation reverberated for all to hear.

His father laughed again. "Foolish girl. He's used to the beatings! They do nothing."

She took a step backward and when Kade didn't move, but stood like a stone statue staring at her, she whirled and raced from the room, from the castle. From his life.

CHAPTER EIGHT

Lightning lit the sky in the distance, forking over the castle. Lia ran down the road, away from the castle, away from Kade. Sobs shook her body. She felt broken. If he loved her, he would never have given the parchment to his father. He knew how much it meant to her! He made her believe he loved her, that he could love her, and then…

She wanted to wail and shout and scream. But she couldn't. She just couldn't. She was too stunned to even bring forth a cry of anguish. This was her fault. She had believed he loved her. And she had loved him. With all her foolish, silly heart. How could she open her heart to such a callous, lying…?

She stumbled and almost fell, but caught herself against a tree. Stupid, she berated herself.

She should have known. She should have known he could never truly love her. No one could. How could she ever have known how deceitful others could be? Maeve raised her to be trusting of others.

A soft rumble of thunder chastised her. She should have known. She wiped the tears from her cheeks, from her eyes. She looked back at the castle. Still, the way he had kissed her with such tenderness, the way he held her in the safety of his strong arms. That had all felt so real, so honest.

How could she have known?

A sob welled inside her and she pushed herself from the tree to continue down the road. She only had one place to go. Home. To Maeve. The only person to ever have truly loved her.

When she turned up the road toward the cruck, she paused at the spot she had found Sir de Rolleston. She looked into the forest, seeing the knight in her mind's eye. "I failed you," she whispered. "I'm sorry."

The wind gusted, swirling her skirts about her legs, tossing her long hair in every direction. She resisted the wind, staring at the spot the knight took his last breath. He would be disappointed in her. He would be angry that his entire life, his mission to keep that parchment safe, had failed when he gave it to her.

She stood that way, fighting the wind, until the large drops of rain began to pelt the earth around her. Punishing in their severity, they pummeled her head, her body. She turned and continued up the road, walking. The rain hid her tears, and this was a good thing. Maeve would not know she was crying. Lia didn't want Maeve to know what had happened, not about the parchment, not about Kade. She didn't want her mother to know how utterly incompetent and foolish she was for believing in him.

By the time the cruck came into view, Lia was drenched. Sheets of rain blew, pushing her toward her home. She stopped. What would she say to Maeve? What lie would she invent? Lia's shoulders drooped. She couldn't do it. She had to tell Maeve the truth, no matter how much she didn't want to. She yearned for Maeve's comfort.

She hurried toward the cruck and reached for the door. The door opened.

Kade stood there.

Lia blinked. Surely, she was imagining him. He could not really be there. She blinked again, but the rain blinded her. She brushed her hair and the rain from her eyes. Still, Kade stood before her.

He reached for her, grabbed her shoulders, and pulled her against him.

The wind quieted, and the gusts of rain stopped to a mere mist. For a moment, she stood, stunned, and scared. She must be mad. This must be Maeve holding her.

"Lia," he whispered against her hair.

His voice rumbled through her like thunder. She recognized his musky scent, the scent of fire and ale. She shook her head and pushed away. "No." This couldn't be. He was at the castle. With his family.

He took her face in his hands, his gaze moving over her, touching every spot. "I was so worried. I thought –"

She shook her head and pulled away from him. "You gave it to your father," she accused, her voice cracking. "You said never."

His gaze turned tender and soft and sympathetic. "And I meant it." He reached into his tunic and pulled out a parchment. A parchment that looked like the one he had given his father. "Did you really think I would give it to him?"

Lia frowned in confusion.

He held it out to her.

Lia took it and opened it. She stared at the squiggles and the lines on the parchment. "I can't read it."

"*This* is the parchment Father wanted."

"But I saw you give it to him."

"You saw me give him *a* parchment. I left you here and went to Father Stephen. I knew he had ink and quill. I know how to write, Lia. I wrote on a second parchment. I changed all the names to fake knights. To knights who don't exist."

Lia looked at the parchment. "This is the real parchment?"

Kade smiled. "My father will be chasing those treasures until he dies."

Lia's heart blossomed with joy. She looked up at Kade, at his sparkling blue eyes.

"I would never betray you, Lia."

Lia threw her arms around his neck and kissed his lips. "Oh, Kade!" Her heart was full of love for him. She pulled back to look at him. "You did this for me?"

"I did this for us," he admitted. "For our future."

"Future?"

"I love you, Lia. And after I marry you, I didn't want to have to look over my shoulder for my father's return."

"Marry?" she echoed.

His smile was warm and loving. "Of course, I'm going to marry you. That's what a man and woman do who are in love." His smile suddenly vanished. "You do love me, don't you?"

Tears rose in her eyes, blurring her vision of him. She wiped them away quickly, not wanting anything to obscure her vision of him. How could she have thought he didn't love her one moment and the very next that he did? She trailed her hand up his muscular arm to his shoulder, her entire body warm and alive. "I've never loved anyone the way I love you. Yes. I love you, Kade. I love you."

He pulled her against him, kissing her lips hungrily.

Maeve stood near the hearth, stirring a pot. She grinned happily.

EPILOGUE

Kade knelt opposite Lia. He stared down into a hole he had dug. "I thought it appropriate to bury it here." It was where Sir de Rolleston died. The trees arched over their heads, blowing gently in the wind.

Lia nodded. "His spirit can watch over it."

Kade lifted the lid of the stone box he brought.

"Are you certain?" Lia asked. "I know how much that box means to you. It was your mother's."

Kade nodded. The stone box was etched with elaborate scrolling and painted with rich red and blue colors. "I'm certain." For him, it was a burial he had not been there for.

Lia dropped the parchment into the box without another word.

Kade replaced the lid and carefully set it into the small hole. He stared down for a long moment. That parchment had caused him a lot of trouble, but in the end, it had caused much more joy. He looked up at Lia. She was staring at him with those clear, clear blue eyes. He grinned at her, and together they pushed the dirt into the hole, covering the stone box.

When they were done, Kade stood and held a hand out to Lia. She nodded once and took his hand, rising to her feet.

"Oh!" she cried and pushed some leaves and twigs over the freshly dug dirt to further hide it from unwanted detection.

She was smart. That was one of the reasons he loved her so. Kade took her hand and pulled her against him. He stared down at her smooth skin, her large eyes, and those full lips. She had healed his wounded and tortured spirit; she had given him a reason to fight his father and to win. He was so grateful he had found her. He lowered his lips to hers, brushing his against her softness.

She truly was his treasure.

The End

ABOUT LAUREL O'DONNELL

Critically acclaimed novelist Laurel O'Donnell sold her first book, **The Angel and the Prince**, to Kensington after being a Romance Writers of America's Golden Heart finalist. She has gone on to win many more awards including the Holt Medallion Award for **A Knight of Honor** and the International Digital Award for **Angel's Assassin.**

Born in Chicago, Illinois, Laurel began writing in junior high school when she carried a pen and paper around wherever she went. In college, she took fiction writing classes to further her skill. Her love of the medieval time period led her to work at King Richard's Faire in Wisconsin where she learned stage combat and sword fighting. The Faire fed her insatiable appetite for the medieval era.

Laurel has many books yet to write and hopes you will join her on her journey to bring the medieval era to life!

Please visit her at her website www.laurel-odonnell.com for the latest information about upcoming releases, contests, and to contact her.

Made in the USA
Las Vegas, NV
22 January 2021